Liana Enli

#IfYouWereHere

Copyright © 2025, All rights reserved.

Any reproduction, copying, or reference to this work, in whole or in part, is strictly prohibited without permission. Citations from the book must be made with mentions of the author.

Liana Enli

ACKNOWLEDGEMENTS

Writing a book is never a solitary journey, and I am deeply grateful to everyone who supported me along the way.

First and foremost, I want to thank my family for their unwavering encouragement and belief in my writing, even when I doubted myself. Your love and support made all the difference. Especially my mom, who was always supporting me in my creativity.

To my friends, who listened to my endless brainstorming sessions and provided invaluable feedback—your insights and honesty helped shape this book into what it is today.

To my early readers and editors, your keen eyes and thoughtful critiques were essential in bringing this book to life. Special thanks to my law classmates Maria & Arpine for helping me with my final cover decision while doing their evidence class.

Finally, to my readers—thank you for picking up this book. Your support means everything, and I hope this story resonates with you in some way.

This book is not about what life is, how to live it, or who is right. This is a story in which real-life episodes occur in different people's lives. Though all of this is united in one character, those separate episodes will make them visible.

***

It is said that the person finds themselves when they depart from everything…

While everyone was busy with their daily business, I kept trying to get involved in my daily routine and dispel my thoughts of self–isolation with my active lifestyle, putting tasks in front of myself that sometimes were artificial.

It was morning. I left home as usual and was heading to work. And though I walked the same road every day, I never noticed the wooded area next to the street. That day, my attention was drawn by the golden retriever dog running toward the forest. Looking around and not seeing the owner, I ran after the dog, thinking he was lost. Diving deep into the greenwood and carefully getting rid of the lush branches, I found myself in a place where there was a small, secluded area with large trees growing upwards. Besides the dog, I also found a 7-year-old white-haired, white-skinned boy who bowed to the dog and stroked him.

"Is it your dog?" I asked the boy, inhaling my breath.

"Yeah," he said, raising his head and stroking the dog.

"It is good. I thought he was lost. You are not lost, are you?" I asked with a smile.

"He always finds me; we are always together; he is my closest friend. And who is your closest friend?" asked the boy curiously.

"Hmmm… Let me think; you're asking a difficult question," I began to remember the people with whom I am close, just like the boy and the dog. I knelt and continued the conversation.

"Probably with no one. Already, no one. In my childhood, I had many friends with whom I thought we were very close, but over time, everyone is gone with their personal lives, and now, as I look at you and your friend, I realize I don't have such a loyal friend who will find me everywhere."

"It's okay, don't be sad, because you've found us, we will become your friends from now on. Right, Sky?" turning to his dog, the boy said, looking at my sad face.

I smiled, stroked the dog, and continued smiling.

"I will only be happy to have loyal friends like you. Are you alone here?" I asked, looking around, not noticing anyone.

"They're there. They are waiting for us," he pointed out the other side of the forest, and I had not yet managed to get my head back from the direction he pointed; he got up quickly and ran with the dog.

"Wait! I can't reach you," I shouted, smiling, and ran after them.

I didn't see them when I left the forest like I had never seen one. Thinking that the boy might have been gone with his parents, I smiled sadly and continued to walk to work.

All day, I remembered that boy with

his dog and the boy's words that we are friends from now on, and a sad smile came to my face.

In the evening, I had a phone conversation with my friend. I was at home, changing clothes in my room.

"I can never forget that wonderful boy; he appeared suddenly and seemed very close to me."

"Well, you've never been indifferent to

the kids and the dogs. You've always wanted a dog, haven't you?"

"Yes, but this boy is not coming out of my head, and I don't even know his name."

"It's okay, our town is so small, you will see him again."

"I hope. And I won't forget to ask for his

name then."

I finished the conversation smiling, turned off the phone, opened the bed cover, jumped in, and fell asleep.

The next morning, I was back to my daily work when I heard already my favorite voices from the playground at the corner of the road … "Sky, Sky, come to me".

They were my new friends. A wide smile appeared on my face, and as if I had seen my loved ones, I hurried up to approach them. The boy was swinging.

"And I've found you again, or you've found me?" I started.

"We wanted you to find us," said the boy and continued to swing.

"And are you alone again?" I asked, looking around.

"You're with us," was the wise answer.

"It's a pity, I've got to go to work."

"If you don't want to go, why are you going?" the boy asked curiously.

"It's a responsibility; we just have to do many things in our lives so that we can live," I told him, going on my knees and sighing.

"And me, not, now I just want to swing."

"I wish it was all so easy, and we would all just swing."

"And if you don't go to work, can't you make a living?" the boy asked.

"I can live, but with great difficulty."

"But you will get a swing instead, will you?"

"You're right," I smiled and continued, "I'll manage to do lots of things, but there is always a fear that you will not be able or manage to do something or will do something wrong."

"And what would you like to do, or what should you do wrong?" the boy asked again curiously and didn't stop to swing.

"You're asking such clever questions that I think I'm talking to an aged man."

"And I'm aged; it doesn't matter that I'm swinging."

"You're right again; there was a time I also

loved swinging."

"And what do you want to do now?" the boy repeated his question.

"Okay. Let me tell you, anyway, I know you won't tell anyone."

"I won't tell anyone. I promise."

"The thing is that I don't know what I want to do now; I just know that I don't want to do what I do now," I said, hanging my head and stroking the dog next to the boy.

"Don't do it! If you keep doing what you don't want to, you will never know what you want to do," the boy said, starting to swing harder.

"I can't do anything. In adults, you need to do something even if you want to swing. For example, to make money, work, and smile at people you don't know. Time is precious, and we must do as much as possible."

"Well, then swing! Why don't you do it if you already know you want to do that?"

"Maybe I should learn from you. You do what you want, and you're happy. You have a friend who is always by your side, and you're never alone. You're just swinging, and nothing can distract you," I said, continuing to stroke the dog.

"Do you want to swing?" said the boy, raising his head and looking at me.

"Yes," after pausing for a moment, I said with a smile.

The boy immediately jumped up, giving me a place. I sat down, and the boy ran back and started rocking me. I was smiling. And every time I gained momentum and looked up to the sky, I felt free and happier. I was overwhelmed by thoughts from my life, childhood, and past road, full of difficulties, obstacles, and choices.

And remembering where I am now and where I came from, I thought about what would happen if I went in a completely different direction and lived a different life. And in those thoughts, I felt that I was slowing down. Paying attention to the child, I noticed how he quickly jumped and ran with the dog. And before I would stop to get down and reach the boy, he disappeared with the dog.

"And again, I let him go, not knowing his name," I told myself loud and angry.

And the thoughts began to flow... what if the reality in which I've lived won't be...what would I do, where would I be, what would I have… a sense of peace that I was constantly trying to pursue myself, as two lives were struggling inside of me...one accustomed to what the society dictates, the environment in which you have to be, and the one I've created by my unbreakable dreams... and this struggle is endless until you find a state that does not give what you can have, but what you need to have.

And again, morning. This time, I decided to sit on my balcony and drink an iced juice while investigating the passers-by. The heat coming from the streets, mixed with the smell of garbage, closed the beautiful view. Everything had become very tiring. The only thing I wanted to do was to run away. But I was still scared to do it alone. I had an insatiable desire to disappear somewhere, relax from everything, to find what I was missing. And the power of attraction made me receive a message from one of my old friends.

"Hello, have you forgotten me?" my friend Alex wrote, a hint of sadness lingering between the words.

"So you gave me a reason," I replied curtly, willing to play with him a little.

"I want to correct my mistake and see you." he hinted, his words laced with regret.

"You can," I said, pausing to see if he would continue.

"Let's go somewhere, only you and me, in the lap of nature," he suggested, his tone soft, almost pleading.

"Won't you get bored with me alone? Let's go with friends," I replied, testing him, my eyebrow raised.

"I don't like many people," he said flatly.

"Me too, but just think—only you and I—if we go, we'll have nothing to do in a few hours, and we'll get bored," I reasoned, unsure of his intent.

"There's a lot to do; don't think about it," he insisted, his determination palpable.

"You didn't convince me," I countered, my voice steady but not entirely dismissive.

"Okay, whatever you want," he replied casually as if he had all the time in the world.

"How easy it is to convince you," I remarked, trying to restart the conversation, feeling a mix of frustration and amusement.

"Okay, I've changed my mind. We're going," he responded with a sudden firmness.

"Are you sure?" I asked, surprised by his quick decision.

"I'm sure," he confirmed, his confidence unwavering.

"Well, then, let's go," I said, relenting.

"Tomorrow?" he suggested eagerly.

"So fast?" I replied, taken aback by his urgency.

"Yes, there is no time," he wrote, his words rushing in like a wave, pushing me to act.

The texts from him were flowing, and the pressure was building. Considering that, in truth, nothing in my overloaded workflow would change today, tomorrow, or even a week later, there was no real reason to delay it until next time. That's why, against my usual instincts, I finally decided to do what I wouldn't normally do.

"Yes," I typed, sealing my decision with a single word.

I made only one backpack when he came. I wanted to be as light as possible!

"And I was expecting more," he began, smiling as he saw my backpack.

"I have warned you that many of your expectations will not be met, so you have one last chance to think," I said, smiling.

"You won't convince me we're going," he smiled, took the bag from my hand, put it in the car, opened the door, and invited me in a very gentle move to sit in the car - at least he is a gentleman.

And here we are on the way. In fact, along the way, thoughts are heard louder and louder, and the dialogue inside can even be heard in some moments.

Alex was one of those people who loved to talk, focus on things, and make jokes.

Although our trip was completely friendly, I was careful with him anyway because nothing was definitive.

By getting there, a beautiful view opened up in front of us, covered with trees and white sand, and little by little, blue-green waves were noticeable.

Before entering the water, we decided to eat and talk.

"Life consists of moments you should enjoy as profoundly as possible," he began, his voice soft but certain.

"I agree, but with wisdom and seriousness," I continued, meeting his gaze, trying to balance his carefree outlook.

"For this moment, being serious doesn't matter; it's more important to enjoy... without losing even a second," he said, his tone growing more insistent as if time was slipping away.

"Do you want to say that short feelings are more important to you?" I asked, curious yet concerned, tilting my head slightly.

"Yes, because I do not expect a long-term continuation of anything," he said clearly, with a finality that made me pause.

"And relationships?" I probed, trying to push him for deeper thoughts.

"I look at everything differently. I don't need a connection at the moment. It is only a restriction. But I'm romantic," he added with a slight, wistful smile.

"And what is the state of 'romantic' for you?" I asked, leaning in, genuinely intrigued by his definition.

"For example, this music," he said, turning on a slow, beautiful song that filled us with a gentle melody.

"It is beautiful. But this is not 'romantic' for me," I replied, shaking my head slightly, feeling disconnected from his interpretation.

"And what does 'romantic' mean for you?" he asked, his eyes curious, searching mine for an answer.

"Crazy things that you would do only with the person you want to have by your side. Craziness, inexplicable things, for example, sticking your head out of a window in a fast-moving car when it is raining outside, and the raindrops seem to be hitting your face."

"Then you say you're not romantic," he said, a playful glint in his eyes and continuing, "You're just pretending to be cold."

"What do you want to do now? Right now," I asked, trying to intrigue him, my tone slightly teasing.

"Are you serious?" he asked, surprised, raising an eyebrow.

"Yes, whatever you answer, I will not be offended," I replied, maintaining a calm but curious expression.

"I'd like to kiss you," he admitted, his voice dropping slightly, testing me.

"What if I don't want to?" I countered, still checking his intentions, my tone cool.

"It's your choice," he said seriously, his playfulness giving way to sincerity.

"Do you mean you will do nothing?" I added, watching his reaction closely.

"Yes, I will not do anything, even if I want to," he said, his voice firm, eyes steady on mine.

"Do you want to say that men can control their desires?" I asked, now probing deeper, curiosity edging my words.

"I don't know, honestly, what kind of guys you've met before me, but if I say something,

I do it, and I can control myself," he replied, a touch of pride in his voice.

"Well, we'll check," I said, challenging him with a half-smile.

"Do you mean you're going to make me want to kiss you, and I won't be able to restrain myself?" he asked, his voice growing playful again.

"Let's see," I teased back.

"No, tell me, can you?" he insisted, leaning in slightly.

"Of course," I answered confidently.

"You can't," he said, smirking.

"I can," I shot back, meeting his gaze directly.

"Have you ever heard that words, as evidence, always require action?" he asked, his eyes glinting with challenge.

"I know," I responded, a sly smile forming on my lips.

"So? Will you prove it?" he asked in his curious and confident tone.

"Let's see, but you have to promise it will be as you said," I repeated, not backing down.

"Don't worry about me. I've already said that what I have said is exact," he replied confidently. However, a trace of skepticism lingered in his eyes.

"All right," I said, locking eyes with him, and we smiled at each other, the tension between us thickening.

"Let's dance now," he said suddenly, extending his hand to me, his eyes softening.

What I liked about him that he was spontaneous, I reached out to him, and we started dancing in the sand. The sand was so soft that it seemed we were rolling deep. He danced well, of course as we met each other during one of his latin events. And I had to get into the role because he challenged me. On the other hand, I wanted to prove to myself that I could because I always considered myself unattractive and not sexy. And such inferiority, which often happens to girls aged 20-30, always closes from the inside, as if every time it strikes and restrains. And since one of my goals was to fully discover, open up my inner world, and discover my abilities, I did my best to put myself to the test.

I have never danced so freely. I tried

my best to keep myself free and to dance inside. The dance that seems to be life, the one you live in…. in dance, it is always visible and more beautiful. I tried to turn off my consciousness, which is always disturbing and restraining, and to close my eyes to imagine a situation that is mine but will never be mine because, in reality, it does not exist and comes only when I dance, with eyes closed. And it was this state of mind that made him come closer to me.

"What? Are you giving up?" I began.

"No," he said in a clear voice.

"Well, let's keep dancing then."

We continued to dance. No matter how much I "warmed" him up, I tried to keep the distance and keep going. And when

I felt he was getting closer, just one kiss away, I decided to stop. My mission was complete and again I have proved to myself that I should never believe in a world of men.

"I want to walk for a while. Will you let me?" I stopped dancing and said with a smile.

"Of course. And I'll be here," he said in a sad voice.

I smiled and went close to the waves. Waves have always been the readers of my thoughts. I see my thoughts more clearly, incomprehensible, and suspicious whenever I look at them, and I feel inner peace.

At this moment, I was standing in front of them lost. I felt that something was overwhelming, but I couldn't understand it. It's always easier when you know what's wrong, but I didn't know anything then. All I knew was that I needed a change. I must make crucial decisions, be more self-confident, and find what is missing inside. Oh, if you were here at that moment.

And I was walking, breathing the fresh smell of the waves mixed with the wind, and nothing else was important to me. I noticed he was looking at me intently and probably going crazy. I imagine... A girl playing with the sand, with her eyes closed, and walking alone on the shore. At least she's crazy!

I walked quite a distance when I saw a

golden retriever running towards me. Yes, he recognized me. I bent down to pet him and looked around to find his little friend. After all, they are always together. And it hadn't taken long.

Immersed in the sand, he built a castle on the shore. I got up happily and walked with the dog to the boy.

"It's a destiny to see each other every day," I began, approaching him and smiling.

"So that we don't miss each other," he said, smiling, raising his head and holding the small shovel.

"What are you building?" I asked curiously, leaning toward the sand.

"A castle," he replied excitedly and continued to build.

"Very beautiful."

"It's a big room where everyone gathers, and here's a place to keep horses," he said, pointing to different parts of the castle.

"So, there are also horses in the castle?" I asked with a smile.

"Of course, otherwise, how will we go for a ride?"

"Perfect. You have thought of everything."

"Yes. And this castle is yours. I gift it to you."

"Are you giving it to me?" I said excitedly.

"Yes. There is a beautiful room for you here. A prince, too. All girls love princes," he began to explain with childish naivety.

"You're right, they love," I said, keeping my excitement.

"Do you already have a prince?" he asked.

"No, I'm still looking for one."

"And who is that man?" he asked, pointing to Alex, looking at me from a distance.

"He's just a friend, so I don't be alone here," I said, looking at Alex.

"Why is he not your prince?" he asked.

"Because... maybe... hmm ... I still don't trust him... he hasn't given me stars yet and made me romantic," I replied with difficulty.

"Why?" he asked again.

"Now that I'm talking to you, I feel like I'm talking to a big man again, and it's crazy," I said, shaking my head.

"As I've said, I'm big. I understand everything. Tell me why you don't trust him and why you came with him if you don't trust him?" the boy asked.

"You asked a very good question. I don't know how you will understand my sharing, but let me tell you something. For adults, everything is based on trust. In other words, you can't consider someone your "prince" until you test him in different situations and make sure that he is the one who suits you, compliments you, and, most importantly, is kind and sincere," I explained.

"Isn't he kind?" the boy asked again.

"Whether he is or he is not kind, I'll find out soon. Today, we are playing a game with him, and we will see who wins," I said.

"You will definitely win," said the boy.

"Really? Why?" I asked.

"Because you are kind and sincere."

"You're so nice," I said excitedly again.

"I know."

"All right, now I've got to go; otherwise, that boy will definitely not be my prince, and he will run away due to loneliness," I hurried, seeing that Alex was already standing and looking at me.

We said goodbye to each other, and I went to Alex.

"Did your talk with the waves go well?" began Alex, smiling.

"Pretty enough. It was nice."

"And what did they say?"

"They said it was worth dancing together for a while again; what would you say?"

"With pleasure."

And he quickly turned on the music, and we started dancing. The boy's words were ringing in my head. He gave me a whole castle.

There was a silence in my head. Yes, there are times when you switch off your head and feel nothing, no matter how much noise there is around you. At that moment, I disconnected my heart from my brain. I wanted to enjoy the moment because I was sure it would never happen again, and I would never do this again. And the closer I got to him, the more I realized he left me with an open space.

One has to work hard to reach a level where any inner impulse can give the right interpretation and understand the real desire.

And I didn't seem ready for that yet. How can you tell if it's yours if you haven't figured out what you need?!

I was left with only a wish from this - to return to that beautiful place again, this time alone.

Say goodbye ... and do it so that there is no desire to meet again ... it has always been my strong point... and the trick is to make the other person understand that he does not want to continue, that there is no reason and is impossible beyond that. How? With conversations. When you take a person to the level where he understands, there is no other way.

"It was a great day, thank you for the invitation," I began.

"Likewise, we'll do it again," he continued.

"Unfortunately, I will return to work from now on, and I will not have such free time," was my answer trying to make him see that he is wasting his time with me.

"Never?"

"About six months, for sure."

"It's a pity; I was already planning where we will go next."

"It's okay; I'm sure you will have a good time there without me."

"Well, I don't have any other choice," was his sad answer, but he already got that he is not okey with my busy lifestyle.

"You will get the best choice, I'm sure," I smiled at him and got out of the car. And yes, he was a gentleman even in the end by holding the door for me.

The next day was like all the other days, making me think about what I wanted from life in general.

Something had to be done urgently. But this time for permanent change and clarity.

And, of course, in any case, the right solution comes in solitude.

"I want to go on a week-long trip," I shared

my thoughts on my wish with my friend An during a meeting in a cafe in the evening.

"Why? Where?" she asked with surprise.

"To get answers to many questions, and the direction... I just want to go a long way, wherever it will take me, that's my right place."

"I can help you with that," she said.

"Really? And how?" I asked impatiently.

"A tour includes three beautiful places in 7 days, including forest, yoga, and waterfall."

"Perfect! It seems like exactly what I need right now. And the conditions?"

"There is only one condition. This whole trip is free of charge, a gift from me, but my boyfriend and I are also joining. We promise to be invisible and not to disturb you," she said with a smile.

"Of course, you can join. But for free? I can't accept such a gift."

"Don't worry, because my boyfriend is the director of a travel company. It's at the organization's expense, which is a business trip for him – a complete rest for us. So, what would you say? Just hurry up; I must confirm by tomorrow," she said excitedly.

"I don't know."

"Are you still thinking? No, this time it's up to me to decide, yes, you're coming."

I decided to obey for the first time in my life, especially since I would be with people close to me.

And in two days, we were on our way.

I have always wanted to travel by car from city to city, country to country. Especially when, after only 3-5 hours, you can end up in another country.

And do you know what was the most interesting? I was enjoying watching the relationship between my friend and her boyfriend. They were so delicate. All along the way, they held hands and sang songs as if in a movie.

At that moment, I wondered what is the real appearance of love. We may be tender to our loved ones, even to animals, but is that the same tenderness and delicacy you give to the person you love? Is just hugging and kissing a delicacy? Is just holding hands a delicacy?

I don't know, but I saw the delicacy in them that I had never seen in any context. And that delicacy was in their eyes. They were so tender, so warm. They were indescribably caring. Every time they looked at each other, it was as if their minds were moving to infinity, and they were disconnected from everything and felt only the existence of one another. Anyway, I thought that was so, and I'm never wrong. Desirable delicacy…

It had been about three hours, and it was time to stop and dine. Two hours left before we reached our destination, and we parked in a beautiful cafe on the way with a retro interior.

We sat down and started ordering, and

while my beloved couple went to order, I sat down at the table and listened to country music. And suddenly I saw a little man running towards me. Is it a coincidence again? It was again my little friend with ice cream in his hand. He just came running and sat next to me.

"Hello, we met again," he began.

"Hello, I'm not surprised by our meetings anymore. You have become my destiny, and I am happier and happier to see you every time," I said with a smile.

"I'm happy too, and Sky is waiting outside," he said, pointing to the dog waiting on the other side of the window.

"What are you doing here?" I asked.

"I'm going on a trip," answered my little

friend eating ice-cream.

"Where?"

"I don't know, but I was told there are 2 hours left."

"How I want to find out that we are going to the same place."

"Me too," replied the boy, eating the ice cream.

"And where are your parents?" I asked.

"They went to the restroom."

"Good."

"Are you alone here?" the boy asked me.

"No, with my friends," I said, pointing to the couple holding hands.

"They look as if they are kids," he said looking at them.

"Why?" I asked with a smile.

"Well, they're holding hands," he said childishly.

"Hmmm... but they are beautiful, aren't they?"

"Very much, he is her prince."

"You're right."

"But one thing is missing."

"What?"

"I won't say."

"Say."

"No, I have to go."

"All right, run." seeing that my friends were already returning, I said goodbye to the boy.

We had a delicious meal and got on the road. And again, the words of my little friend were all over my mind. What was missing...? and in fact, love turns us into kids!

A kid... maybe it's because you're starting to do things that you don't think the one will misunderstand, because the person next to you is the one who wants to see you like that... the way you won't be with anyone else... to see your freedom... the manifestation of your inner world, which is closed to everyone else... and all this exists when you are not afraid... you are not scared of losing your opponent by opening your inner world to him... and you do things that make you happy, like a small stubborn child. And what can be lacking in all this?

And here we reached our first destination. The city was really beautiful with its old architecture and cozy corners. After staying at the hotel, I left the beautiful couple alone. I took a short walk to see as much as possible in the new environment.

The most interesting thing is that frequently, we look for what is right next to us only because we try to keep away from us what is ours, what we like, what is for us, what is dear to us, and what is in us... to drive it away and not let it in...

I felt like I wasn't alone, as if everywhere I went, I was accompanied by someone who sometimes was touching my hand, trying to catch me. In my mind, I was wandering down one of the narrow streets when I suddenly came across a young man in the corner. We hit each other. He managed to grab me by the shoulders and gently not let me fall.

"I'm not saying sorry, and instead of that, I want to invite you to a music party to prove that our clash was not accidental," the young man said with a confident, calm voice.

"Why do you think I like music and have no other plans for tonight?" I replied, smiling and standing with him.

"It is possible to change any plan if you have a good offer. And then, I think, you won't refuse to see what you haven't seen yet," he continued ingeniously.

I just smiled and walked my way.

"Promise me you will accept my apology," he shouted after me.

I looked back, smiled, turned my head left and right, and continued walking.

I wondered what kind of person he was and how he could be so direct and easy with strangers. No one would ever apologize like that. And he did.

And regardless of my silence, of course, I decided from the very first moment that I would accept the invitation and spend the evening with my friends at the address which he quickly wrote on a piece of paper and put it in my hand during the conversation.

It was evening. As soon as I returned

to the hotel, I informed my friends about the invitation, and we went out two hours later.

The place was on the roof, in an abstract style, with beautiful lights and outdoor wooden chairs. In the middle was the stage where the band was playing. We settled down not far from the stage and started enjoying the music.

Suddenly, I saw a familiar face. The same young man who almost threw me down. He had not seen me. I began to study him carefully. During the first meeting, I did not notice his slender posture. However, at the same time, his delicate posture could be seen in his look, and I was still afraid to look into his eyes. And his fingers were so tenderly embracing the guitar as if they were one body ... his smile, his searching look for something, his movements…

I turned off my brain and listened to how he made those beautiful sounds out of the guitar, and when I closed my eyes, it was as if I could feel his touch again when he caught me…

The play was over... I quickly turned around so he wouldn't notice me. I saw him come down from the stage and go to his friends.

We were talking with my friends when my eyes fell on the roof's edge, where I noticed a boy and immediately likened him to my little old friend. "But it was impossible, here?" I got up to get closer to him and check because seeing him here would also be very interesting.

Reaching the end, I turned the boy over with my hand, and, yes, it was him.

"No way, you're following me," I said with a happy smile, feeling surprised but secretly pleased.

"Well, if we play now, I'll find you again," he replied with a childish grin, his playful energy infectious.

"What are you doing here?" I asked, my curiosity getting the better of me.

"What you do—listening to music," he said, tilting his head slightly as if it were the most natural thing in the world.

"And did you like it?" I inquired, leaning in a little, curious about his taste.

"I like the guitar," he replied, his eyes lighting up, continuing, "and you?"

"Me too. It calms me down," I said softly, feeling our gentle connection grow.

"I want to learn to play guitar," the kid said with a bright smile, his eyes full of excitement.

"What's the matter? You can," I said encouragingly, and continued, "Moreover, I'm pretty sure I know the guitarist who's playing right now, and I could ask him to give you some lessons."

"That guy?" the boy asked, pointing toward a young man nearby.

I turned to see who he was referring to and realized it was him. Smiling, I continued, "Yes, him. He played well, didn't he?"

"Yeah. He's good," the boy replied, nodding in approval.

"Do you know him?" I asked, surprised by the boy's confident statement.

"No, but since you like him, he must be good," the boy said with a grin, his childlike logic catching me off guard.

"And who said I liked him?" I asked, genuinely surprised by his observation.

"Because I saw how you looked at him," he said innocently as if it was the most obvious thing in the world.

"You're wrong," I said, laughing softly. "I don't even know him."

"But why?" he asked, his curiosity piqued.

"Because we met only today, and there was no time or occasion to get to know him," I explained, amused by the child's questioning.

"Do you want to know him?" he asked, tilting his head, his innocent curiosity making me smile.

"I don't know. I'm leaving in 3 days; I heard him here; it was nice; I think that's enough."

"And you don't want to see him in your life, never, ever?" he asked with great interest.

"I don't know. To understand whether I want to see him in life, I must first get to know him better."

"Well, now you have a chance to do it because he's coming here," he said, pointing to the young man.

I turned in the direction of his finger, and he stood directly in front of me; when I turned the boy back again, he was no longer there, as if he had disappeared.

"Are you looking for something? It seems that the only person who should look for something is me," he said with a smile and a calm voice.

"What are you looking for?" I said, looking at him.

"I have already found what I am looking for from the moment I came here.

"I'm happy for you," I said, and I wanted to go to my friends.

"It's not fair," he said, holding my hand and not letting me go.

"What's not fair?" I said, looking at his hand holding my hand.

"You haven't apologized to me yet."

"Should I?" I said, surprised by his stubbornness.

"Well, that would have been fairer because our clash was both our fault; I was in a hurry, and you weren't careful," he said calmly as if that was the case.

"Hmmm... and what apology do you expect from me?" I asked, trying to get into his game.

"Well, equivalent. I invited you somewhere; now it's your turn to invite me," he said impatiently with a smile.

"All right," I said with a smile after a moment of silence, "tomorrow morning at 11 o'clock, we'll meet at the same place where our clash occurred. I hope you remember that place."

"I will never forget it. And where are we going?"

"Wherever you want, unlike you, I will give

you a choice."

"Do you promise we will go where I want?"

"I promise, you know this unknown country better than me."

At that moment, I was convinced that he was harmless to me. At the same time, I was dying of curiosity about his next step, so I decided to give him the right to "take the lead" and be an observer myself.

"Very well, until tomorrow," he said, leaving my hand with a smile, "and don't forget warm clothes."

I heard his last words as I was leaving. I think my return smile gave him my answer.

It was 10:30 in the morning, and I was

walking to our collision place. Aside from the thoughts whether I was right to meet him or not, the little boy I met everywhere did not leave my mind. And every time I met him, something interesting happened to me. I have to talk to him longer next time.

And here I was there. He was already there, leaning on the wall, completely in blue. His jeans jacket filled his body, and he became  more attractive. And his look… It's a pity I still couldn't imagine the color of his eyes.

"At the right time," he began, his gaze steady

as he looked at me.

"I don't like being late," I said confidently, feeling sure of myself.

"In that case, it's time to move so we're not late," he replied, his tone matter-of-fact.

"Where?" I asked a flicker of curiosity in my voice.

"The place I chose," he said, with a hint of mystery.

"And what did you choose?" I pressed, trying to hide my impatience.

"What's the difference for you? You promised to go where I chose. Did you bring warm clothes?" he asked, his voice firm.

"Yes," I said, nodding towards my bag.

"Sit down," he instructed, motioning to the motorcycle on the other side of the wall.

"Are we going to go with this? Can I trust you?" I asked, my voice tinged with apprehension, unsure of what kind of driver he was.

"I think you have no other choice," he said, teasingly smiling. "If you don't trust me now, you won't know if it's worth it," he added, swinging onto the motorcycle and handing me the helmet.

All I could do was silently put on the helmet and sit with him, my heart pounding with excitement and nervousness.

We were running silently, and that silence told me so much that I wanted to ride endlessly.

Suddenly, he accelerated the speed. I grabbed his back tightly as if hugging him. I felt his body, energy, breath, and the sound of a fast-beating heart. It was as if I had caught a relative who was not an acquaintance of yesterday but someone who had always been in my life.

And here, listening to the melodies of the wind, gradually slowed down and reached a part of nature surrounded by tall trees. It was like paradise. I went down  carefully and admiringly, talking off my helmet.

The sun's rays shone around the place,

and the view of the lake in front of it was reminiscent of a cartoon scene.

"Did I choose the right place?" he began.

"Perfectly, it is exactly what is needed," I replied with a delighted look.

"So, I've guessed," he continued.

"What?" I wondered.

"You," he replied with confidence.

"Me?" I asked in surprise.

"Yes, you. I felt right about you."

"You did," I replied with a smile.

"And you must be hungry, let's go further."

He said, pointing to the cover on the

left side of the floor with a basket that he put on the ground when we arrived. We sat down and started eating. We were silent. It was so nice to just be silent with him. His gaze said it all. He was looking and smiling. Then he drew something with his finger on the cover, took the leaves that had fallen to the ground, and made an abstract picture with an irregular arrangement. I followed him carefully, trying to understand him. Then he got up, shook my hand, lifted me, and walked to the lake.

I followed him! He entered a labyrinth beside the lake, surrounded by bushes and beautiful flowers. The most positive thing was that he didn't even try to tear those flowers away and give them to me as if he guessed that I liked seeing the flowers in their place.

Suddenly, I heard a loud stream of water. We reached the river. He was silent. Me too. He began to walk along the river as if he was following it. I followed him! We jumped from stone to stone, trying not to get wet. Sometimes, he looked back to ensure everything was fine with me and that I was going with him. And sometimes, he reached out to help me land softer by jumping from stone to stone.

No sound all the way. Only touch and care. Here, we came to a place where the river seemed to split, and the broken tree at the top seemed to have become a natural bridge. He climbed onto the tree and gave his hand to me. Naturally, I followed him. He helped me get on the tree and sat down next to me. We watched the scene in silence for a few minutes, listening to the sway of each leaf, the river's flow, the sound of birds, and the whisper of the wind. That silence made me close my eyes and take a deep breath, which I did. He just looked at my face and smiled.

"I like coming here," he began after a long pause.

"Why?" I wondered.

"Here, I hear everything and understand

what seems difficult."

"Do you often come here?"

"Unfortunately, not much. But when I do, I return back being a different person; new melodies are born here in my head, and I start to create."

"Even now?"

"Even now… A delicate, tender melody…"

"Will you show me?" I asked with interest and a smile.

"Maybe. Let's see what happens," he said sadly, looking straight ahead.

"What color are your eyes?" I began.

"Haven't you seen it yet?" he wondered.

"I haven't tried."

"Then look at them," he said, bringing his head closer to mine, continuing, "Do you see now?"

"No, because I'm looking at you now, but not at your eyes," was my reply.

"So you're looking at my face, but not into my eyes?" he wondered.

"Yes, I know you think it is crazy, but I can't

look you in the eyes. Why? When you look into a person's eyes, you feel him better, with the whole body, with the whole inside, and because of that, it is very likely that if he gets close to you, you will let him in," was my long answer.

"And what's wrong with that?"

"The fact that, unlike many, if I let him in, there is no other way out, and I will fight at all costs to keep him inside me."

"And how many people have you let in such a way that you still don't want to?"

"I will only say that now there is no place and no time."

"As you wish. And I'm not afraid to let in, not even you," he said in a sad voice, then looking carefully into my eyes, put his hand closer to mine, and I almost felt his touch. He got closer, so I tried to pull over.

He seemed to be playing with me. I was chasing him, and he was coming towards me more; I was trying not to see him; he was forcing me to penetrate his soul.

"I'm not going to touch him ... it's going to bring me closer to him, and he's nobody to me, just a temporary episode that is very beautiful, and now sitting next to me, and I'm feeling so positive that I would hug him and never let him go", the thoughts tormented me. And the silence made everything more loud. He seemed to be planning everything, but at the same time, he was very careful. I could feel his gaze on me and explore his inside, and that's why he didn't even have to talk to me ... he had a weird trick ... I never felt what I felt when he was next to me... it was just inexplicable... as if a part of yours that you had lost and that you know so well that there is no need even to speak... and silence…

It was getting dark... of course, his attempts to approach me failed because my perseverance prevailed.

"It's getting dark," he began, looking at the stars, "Do you like darkness?"

"Yes, in the dark, everything becomes clearer," I began, looking at the stars as well.

"It's interesting," he continued.

"What?"

"You are the only person I have seen who loves to look at the sky so much."

"It's just the only thing that is permanent, and when something appears and disappears in different episodes of your life, at least you can be sure that by looking up, you will see the same thing you saw yesterday or a few days ago, a few years ago, for example, the stars, the moon... they are always in the same place, you can always look at them and feel calm because at least they are in their place."

"So you think there are no other permanent things?"

"Yes, even you are temporary... me... this moment... and in a few years, each of us will be in different places and looking up at the sky, we will see today's moon and stars, and we will just remember this moment with a smile."

"Do you want to say there is no chance we will look at the sky together in a few years?"

"As I said, I do not believe in permanent things."

"All right, we'll see," he said under his breath, and we continued to stare at the stars silently.

"It's already too late," I began after a few minutes of silence.

"And we have no place to hurry," he said calmly, looking at me.

"Aren't we?" I said anxiously.

"We aren't. And now I will tell you the plans for the second half of our day," he said, got up, and went to the motorcycle.

I looked at him and saw him taking out a bag from the side of his motorcycle. Then, he came and started to take something out of it and fasten it to the ground.

"What are you doing?" I asked, getting up.

"I'm making sure we won't get cold at night."

"Why must we catch a cold if we'll be gone soon anyway?"

"And who said we are going to go?" he said, looking at me with a smile, and went on to put something in the ground.

"Of course, it's interesting to see how you fight with these sticks, but please tell me, what are you doing?" I asked, trying to understand his plan.

"As I mentioned, it's time for the second part of my surprise. We will spend the night here today with these stars and the moon. You said you could be with them endlessly."

I froze for a moment, and it was unexpected, and, of course, I didn't want to be alone with him so much.

"Are you kidding? I didn't mean that at all," I tried to persuade him.

"It's too late. Do you remember when I asked how you would like to spend the day? You told me to decide for myself, and our day ended the next morning when we met in town. In other words, we still have one whole night, so why should we waste it in vain? I told you to choose; you allowed me to choose, and this is my choice," he said boldly, continuing his work.

And I didn't know what to say because he was right, and I gave him a chance to choose. Of course, I could argue with him and demand that he take me home, but with that, I would lose my self-confidence and the status I had gained in his eyes. That's why I kept quiet and sat on the cover, watching closely what he was doing.

"Our tent is ready," he said a few minutes later.

"Are we going to stay in the tent?" I asked in surprise, but already reconciled to every thought.

"Of course, it's a good one. It is for four people, and we will make it there with two people," he said with a laugh and moved the items on the floor.

"I think I'll fit in," I said jokingly.

"Well, it is the right time we fit inside because it's already cold outside."

I got up quickly and went into the tent. It was interesting to me because I had never been in a tent in my life, never spent a night there. It was nice.

"What are you thinking about?" he said, looking at me lying motionless.

"I just never imagined this moment with you. We are in the tent, the two of us, you lying next to me... I don't know…"

"If you don't like it, we can get up and go right now," he said and sat down anxiously.

"No, I want to stay. It's nice like this. You also stay," I said, smiling as I lay down, looking at him, seeing how he smiled at what I said and lying beside me.

The tent was really big, and at least more than one person would fit between us, so we each lay in a corner, far away from each other. But he was attracted to me. I have never had such a feeling. I somehow restrained myself from touching him.

"What would you like to do now?" he interrupted my thoughts.

"I don't know, you?" I tried to avoid the question.

"I know what I want to do, and now I'm doing it; tell me, what do you want to do?"

"Honestly, I don't know, I don't understand. Sometimes I feel afraid of understanding," I said sadly.

"I think you know, you just don't want to understand," he said, looking at me.

I was silent. There was no point in saying anything because he was right.

"Will you give me your hand for a minute to check something," I said, filling up the courage.

"If that's your wish, of course," he said, reaching out to me.

I touched it, felt it, understood it, kept silent…

He was silently watching how I was "playing" with his hand.

A few minutes later, I whispered.

"I feel better this way."

"Do you mean you feel me?" he asked skeptically.

"Yes, and I understand."

"Do you know what I want now?"

"I do."

"And what do I want?"

"You have to tell yourself that."

He smiled. I kept holding his hand, and we looked at each other lying down.

"All right, let's go to sleep," I said, slowly letting go of his hand.

"Good night," he said, turning his face to me.

I also turned to him, folded my arms under my "nose" and closed my eyes.

It was so hard to sleep ... after feeling so much. By touching his hand, I let a part of him in, and who knows, was it good or bad?! The thoughts were endless. I was trying to sleep. It got cold. I began to tremble.

Suddenly, I felt his hand on my back, slowly bringing me closer. I did not open my eyes. He thought I was asleep. And finally, he hugged me, leaning firmly on me. I stopped getting cold. He was warming me up. He began to hug me tighter. I kept my eyes closed. He thought I was asleep. Let think so.

Morning... When I woke up, I was

alone in the tent. The ray of the sun had already penetrated and was reaching my eyes. I carefully opened the tent door, pulling the lid as if it could be called that, and the only thing I saw was the silence and the whiteness. Yeah, all that sounds pretty crap to me. It was 7 am. I took a deep breath and went back inside. I lay down and began remembering my feelings at night as his body warmed me. Surprisingly, I have never experienced such a feeling. And that was one of the only things I wanted. But it's already morning, it's over, and the feelings of freedom must be put back in the box before he comes... and nothing seems to have happened.

Suddenly, I heard the sound of walking. It was him. He carefully opened the door and, half entering his hand, walked over to me and began.

"Good morning, I hope you like fruits," he said, smiling and giving me the apple.

"You can't imagine how much I like it," I said happily and began to eat with gusto.

"I hope you slept well. Didn't you catch a cold?" he asked, sitting next to me and taking his feet out of the tent.

"To my surprise, it was very comfortable and warm," I said coldly, trying not to show my feelings.

"It's very good," he said, restraining himself and trying to show him the cold.

His mind had mixed thoughts, like, "Didn't she see or understand…"

Oh, how I wish he understood that "she didn't open her eyes so that she wouldn't understand…". Yes, I was too afraid to open my eyes and see as it was.

And so, after sitting in silence for a while, we got out of the tent, walked for a while, and, getting closer to the lake, turned on the music and by extending his hand, he said with a smile:

"I know these are our last minutes with each other, so let's dance together as a goodbye."

I silently held out my hand, and as if wrapped in the new rays of the sun, we began to dance. I don't even know what kind of dance it was … as if it was a mixture of all the dances … waltz, tango, latino... the only thing I felt or wanted to feel at that moment was that absorbing energy coming from him whenever I touched him... I didn't want to let him go... but to keep him inside me... to feel his whole body... to wrap up... to touch his face and to hear his deep breath and to speed up his heartbeat... I could see the whole thing, but at the same time,

I kept myself away so he wouldn't understand how I felt. It was pointless…

The music ended, and we stopped. For a moment, we just smiled, looked at each other, and went to leave. Sitting on his motorcycle, we drove back, as I had to leave for another city in a few hours.

We were already near my building. He helped me down the aisle, and I gave him the helmet.

There was sadness in our eyes, and even though he tried to not show it completely, I felt he had chosen to hide…

It is the most horrible feeling when you feel that something is left to do, but because you do not fully understand it, you decide to give up and do nothing. I felt that he was also trying to tell me something. Still, something incomprehensible to me kept him from taking a step. It was as if he was playing a role with me, restraining himself, just going back to my reaction at every step, as if he was trying on me or was afraid of me. I wouldn't be surprised if he was afraid. After all, I also played a role with him, and it was difficult for him to understand me. During those two days, he was the one who saw me the most, recognized me, and understood me, but at the same time, I was restrained and controlled the most when I was right next to him. I didn't trust him a few hours ago, and now I trust him more than I do myself. However, we will be moving in opposite directions in a few hours.

"Well, thank you for the day," I began.

"Thank you for trusting me," he continued.

"I had no choice," I said with a smile.

"You always have a choice," he said in a low, sad voice; putting on the helmet, I saw his gaze go out of my eyes.

At that moment, it seemed to me that I was looking and seeing his eyes, the depth, the silence... and he was the first person in whose eyes I dared to look at and see how he was leaving... and nothing would make me forget the silent depth of his eyes… The only time I didn't want to say goodbye…

And I was already in my room, and everything was ready. I stayed a little bit, and we left.

In about 5 hours, we were already in another city. This city was important to me because I had a very close friend with whom we planned to meet that evening. And even though we have planned to go yoga, I have decided to skip it and just relax.

It was around 7 in the evening; we were already accommodated in our hotel when I received an "SMS" saying "Come down, I'm near the hotel." I hurried downstairs, where my friend was already waiting for me. I didn't expect him as we agreed to see each other the next day.

"How glad I am that we finally saw each other here," he began, hugging me.

"Me too, it's a beautiful city," I continued.

"Well, let's go. I'll show you the whole city," he offered.

Although I have decided to stay and relax, something told me to be spontaneous.

And we went out. We walked so much that I memorized every little corner of the city.

We talked about life, the city, work.

He was one of the persons who has seen the world and has a large overview.

"Today is the birthday of one of my colleagues, and he invited me to dinner. What would you say if we went there together?" he began.

"So unexpected, I'm not even dressed right for that occasion," I answered.

"It's okay, be spontaneous, you won't be here any time soon".

"You are right, let's go," I replied, and walked to the way he showed me with a smile.

His friend's apartment was in a 4-floor building, quite big and beautiful. Besides us, about 30 people sang, danced, and drank. A real birthday party. I was there but with my thoughts in the tent.

Sometimes, we meet people to meet other people…

I would never have believed that expression if I had not lived it myself.

I was leaning on the balcony, drinking dry white wine, when suddenly, a glass of wine remained on my lips. In the crowd, talking to each other, I saw him. For a moment, it seemed to me that I was blindfolded or confused with someone else, but once I looked at him again, I was convinced it was him. He saw me. I mean, he saw how I was looking at him frozenly. It was a shame, but it happened automatically, and he left his conversation and came to me with a surprised smile. And the closer he got to me, the more I started to smile... but still frozen and with my glass of wine in the same position.

"If I had been told this tomorrow, I would have considered it unbelievable if I had not been sure that I have not yet drunk any alcohol," he began with humor.

"And I'm trying to drink; maybe that's why I think this is just my imagination," I continued.

"At least one of us believes in miracles; in this case, it's me."

"And how did it happen that just a few hours ago, we said goodbye to each other in another city and found ourselves in the same place?" I asked with a smile.

"Destiny. So we left something unfinished there. We must continue here," he joked.

"You think spending two days together still leaves something unfinished?" I added.

"Not me, but everything seems to be decided for us."

"Do you believe in such things?"

"I believe in everything, in anything I see, and I see this, and I do not mind. And you?"

"What I?"

"Do you mind if we continue what we left unfinished?"

"Well, if something is left unfinished, it should be finished."

"Very good. Well, I'll come now, wait for me."

He said and ran inside. I saw him entering the kitchen, taking a glass and a bottle of wine, and quickly returning to me. Filling his glass, he began.

"Well, let's drink so that nothing is left unfinished, and we finish everything."

"Wonderful toast," I smiled and handed my glass.

A beautiful dance song started to play.

"Oh, I think I know what's left to finish. It's my favorite song, and you have to come with me to understand it," he said, taking the glass of wine from my hand, placing it on the windowsill, and holding my hand against my will, dragging me inside to dance.

And no matter how much I did not want to go and dance, he just "surrounded" me. It was a beautiful song, and slowly, I got into the rhythm. He grabbed my hips and twisted them with gentle touches. Then he looked into my eyes, and I remembered his look at each other; it was the same as when we were saying goodbye. It was the same but now disguised with a bit of color. The song is over. Our eyes stared at each other for a few seconds without words. Feeling how close he was to me, I turned my look and quickly said:

"We have finished what we left unfinished; it is time to breathe fresh air."

I ran to the balcony again, took the wine, took a deep breath, and drank. He came after me and stood behind - standing frozen for a moment.

For a few seconds, we silently stared out at the stars. I felt his thoughts but restrained mine. I wanted to touch him to understand better what he felt that moment, but wouldn't that make things more difficult? His gestures, his look, his silence... they were just turning me on... and the bad thing was that it was exactly what I needed at that moment... but I did not dare to give in to my desire; I did not want to change the rules of the game, I did not want to try to see…

"Let's go for a walk," I began spontaneously, wanting to escape from my thoughts.

"Why? Are you tired of the stars?" he joked.

"The opposite. We will see them better by walking, and then, I think, we will never have such an opportunity to look at the stars together. From tomorrow, we will go to different cities because we have no other unfinished business with each other," I replied to his joke.

"Are you saying you are sure we'll never meet again?" he asked with a smile.

"Well, this is all; I feel that way," was my stupid answer.

After a few seconds of silence, he continued.

"Well, let's get as much as possible from tonight."

He said he extended his hand to me to go out together.

"Wait, let's not forget the wine," he quickly returned with the wine, took the bottle, and we left.

That night was the full moon, one of the moons we used to look at and dream. We hear some sounds, feel strange, and some unusual things in the style of "mystery".

But at that moment, what was happening between me and him was mystical. I was feeling him more and more as if he was letting me in and trying to keep the boundary that would never allow me to get out of there.

We were walking into the empty,

half-wet streets. Hardly anyone would dare to be outside at 2 a.m. after the rain.

We were looking at each other, smiling regularly, and silently walking. And that lasted for a few minutes until he stood up and handed me the bottle and said:

"Don't you want to drink?"

"If you think you can get me drunk, this bottle will not be enough," I joked.

"No, I just felt the need to drink, but if you don't want to, I will drink it by myself," he said, raising the bottle and pouring the wine into his mouth.

"Give me the bottle", I exclaimed with a smile.

He handed me a bottle of wine, I drank, and we continued walking.

"What is your purpose in life?" he began in a half-drunk, serious voice.

"Before, I knew, and I could say what goal I was setting, I was achieving, but now I am a little lost and feel that the goals I set do not suit me; they don't justify me," I answered seriously.

"And why is it like that?"

"Because I have changed, my demands from

life and people have changed."

"And what kind of person are you now?" he wondered.

"You tell me about it," I asked him with a smile, continuing to walk and dance.

"Hmmm, you are asking a difficult question because sometimes you are not what you show to be," he began, thinking and smiling.

"How is that?," I asked with a smile.

"We have met three times, and I have felt you differently thrice. And surely, it's not because I got to know you better each time. It's just that I feel there is a constant change in you. I can't explain how; I can only say that this change is still going on in you, and now we are changing again together... we, because you, in some inexplicable way, are forcing me to change too."

"Tell me, what would you do now if you were me?"

"The same thing you are doing to me now."

"What do I do to you?"

"You are playing."

He said these last words in a sad voice as we came so close to each other and stood motionless in front of each other that we were about to kiss.

I wanted to kiss him at that moment, but something inside did not let me again. It was not the risk that we might not see each other but the possibility that I might want him again and again after that. I will never be able to unbind him from my inside. He was the only person who made me feel some fear, and that's why I tried to make a joke in the situation when there was only one step left for our lips to reach each other. I turned my head, took the wine from his hand, drank it, and ran shouting:

"And nothing will change my desire to drink this wine completely."

He ran after me with a smile. I was running fast. Suddenly, I heard music; I stopped. He was next to me, and looking at my face, he said:

"Are you tired?"

"Shhh, do you hear what good music is playing? Listen carefully! One of my favorites - "Pretty Baby"."

"I'm listening."

He said, approached me, took the bottle of wine from my hand, put it on the ground, took my hand, and we danced. I would say we went around as we were hardly moving because of alcohol. It was a tender and delicate song, and he was moving wonderfully. His every touch was indescribable. I closed my eyes to feel the music better, and the wine was a little bit much to blame for. But I felt safe and calm in his arms... I don't know why, but I completely trusted him. Yes, with him I always wanted to dance in his arms. The feeling that you can't have often.

The song is over. We stopped. Trying to avoid further possible romantic conversation, I started:

"It seems that now I understand what we left unfinished, and I feel we have just finished it."

"Do you think we're done?" he asked sadly.

"Moreover, I think it is time to return."

"Well, if you feel that way, so do I."

He said that in a sad voice and took a bottle of wine from the ground as if getting ready for my sign to move. I felt that there was still something left for him, but at the same time, if I let him get closer to me, it would be impossible to get away from him anymore. The border was guarded. Let him think we are friends.

As a gentleman, he suggested to accompany me home and of course I informed about that to my friend in order he didn't worry.

"Well, it looks like I'm having a "déjà vu", but I'm saying goodbye to you again," he said as we reached our hotel. "Really, let's be sure it won't happen again," I replied with such a stupid smile, blaming me inside for those stupid words.

"Well, we don't have anything else left; good night," he said with a smile.

When I watched him slowly walk away, I wanted to run to him like in a romantic movie and say that we have not finished anything yet. We still have a lot of unfinished things together, but again, the voice from inside, which was ten times stronger, nailed me to close my mouth. And so I gave up again…

The next day was the day of return.

Of course not everything went as planned. It was as if I had been away from my apartment for months, not a week. This journey created a need to reconsider my life. So, the first thing I did was go to the cafe and buy my favorite cappuccino.

It was nice to have coffee in my hand and to walk calmly in places where I always had incomprehensible thoughts while walking. To my surprise, there was nothing in my head at that moment. Only me, cappuccino, my slow steps. And I seem to understand why I felt that way. I learned patience and the ability to wait. Seeing my favorite bench, I decided to take a break and sit down to enjoy the beautiful weather. I had just sat down when I saw a dog licking my hand. I leaned to the side. It was my favorite friend - a retriever. Of course, his friend was not late.

"I was waiting to meet you," I began with a smile as the boy approached.

"We too," the boy said and continued, "and where have you been?"

"Well, after our last meeting, I traveled to several places, and here I am. I guess you arrived a few days ago."

"And where is that boy?" he asked curiously.

"Which boy?" I wondered.

"From the roof."

"He stayed there," I said with a sad smile.

"It is bad. I liked him."

"You didn't even know him; how could you like him?"

"I knew him."

"Well, let's not talk about him; let him remain a story."

"Heroes always find each other in stories," said the boy.

"This is not one of those stories, little one. In this case, the story had already had a beautiful end," I said, smiling and touching his head.

"Well, in any case, the stories are always unfinished," he said with childish naiveté and began to pet the dog.

I smiled and continued.

"And that is why I will go home now and write my new story."

"What are you going to do?" he asked curiously.

"First, I will change my job. I wanted it for a long time, but I just got my courage. Then I will do what I have always wanted to do."

"What?"

"Oh, I'll tell you that the next time we meet, and I'm sure it won't be too late," I said and left.

"All right, we'll be here waiting for you," said the boy.

I left, leaving them on the bench.

That little boy once again reminded me that it was time to write a new story... my own story... with my own hands…

From that moment, I decided that I had to change my life without anyone's help, without looking for anything. After all, the time spent on these questions can be used to build the future. I spent that evening in silence, of course, with thoughts and memories about him. After all, I could see him inside me to some extent, and every second I spent with him was a depth into which I could dive endlessly. And it was that choice between me and him that scared me. Yes, the choice between him and me, because with him, I felt like a different person - before my eyes came the life we could have, but for which I was not yet ready, or I was not sure that what I saw was what he saw too. After all, our lives were so different. We were close souls, but each in search. And as he confessed to me during the last talk, I forced him to look for something and change, which would hinder his self-control. I could not have everything under my control because he was different from everyone. After all, I saw myself in him because he was changing like me; his change was like mine.

But there was one thing that stayed unchanged after meeting him. I saw him every night in my dreams; he hugged me, and those dreams were so vivid that I often didn't distinguish them from reality. They seemed to be my secret reality. But in those dreams, he always left in the end - leaving me alone...

And that is why when your heart says one thing, but your brain says something else, and you don't understand what you want from inside - choose silence... lose... surrender... do nothing... and then what can be heard will be heard... that is what I did...

I spent the next day at home holding a notebook and pen, writing down any thoughts I saw in my future to understand from where to start my story.

It turns out that it is not so difficult when you are focused and isolated from the outside world. No phone calls, no internet. Only you and the notebook.

And by the end of the day, it seemed like I already had a business plan to start my story. It remained to act.

The next few days, I spent running with a few different encounters, and most importantly, in that run, I forgot about any part of my already finished story.

And finally, the day came when I started my own business. It was a fashion brand store where I collaborated with different brands worldwide. It was too early to have my brand yet.

It all started perfectly. I had a small shop with an adjoining office and a few employees. I have long dreamed of entering this field and having my own boutique. Orders were increasing day by day.

As my business grew, so did my quality of life. My daily routine consisted of morning meetings that lasted until late evening. The evenings were full of networking, but with different people who slowly filled my circle of friends, the meetings with them moved to cafes or bars.

I slowly began to feel that I was living, enjoying the day; even mostly working, I felt changed, and in my opinion, for the better. The only thing I missed were my two little friends, the boy and the dog, whom I had not been able to see for several weeks.

Even I met someone in my life who seemed to understand and fit me. We were working together. In other words, I was providing services for their company and slowly becoming friends; our business office meetings were moved to cafes and bars, so we did not understand how we got closer.

It is always like that when you dare to let a person come close to you and open doors for him, you start to know, and a relationship is formed by itself. And yes, any relationship can be built or not built by desire. When you give the other person a chance, you start working on yourself and adapting to the other person. The emergence of that desire for adaptation allows the relationship to develop. I had that desire more than ever, especially since things were going well. I wanted to eliminate only one point in me: the urge to dream and live with fairy tales that were still left from the previous journey.

Everything was different with him; we were going in the same direction, with the same practical mood, and were more mature and purposeful. And I wanted to believe I had finally found someone solid and could count on him.

Three months after our relationship, he offered to rent an apartment together. However, as much as I was obsessed with him and spent the whole day with him, I was still afraid to go to the next level. But everything led to it.

Six months passed without even realizing it. My business has been developing, and I already have a ground in my personal life; everything seems perfect. In addition, we had an invitation to Italy to make a big deal. And since it was a joint project, my boyfriend and I had to be present together.

We were already on the plane when he started:

"I think the deal will happen, and it will bring double profits to our company."

"We will do everything for that," I said, taking his hand.

"If so, we'll open a branch here," he continued, deep in his notebook.

"Definitely. After all, your only goal is to spread your company worldwide."

"Yes, yes, and that is already close."

"But we'll also have time to see Italy, won't we?"

"Let's see if there is time left. Work first of all."

"Of course. But I think we will manage to walk together; we have not been alone for a long time."

"We will be at the hotel. Let's see what we can manage."

"All right," I said sadly, leaning back in my chair and looking through the window at the sky and the clouds.

I have always compared looking at the sky from the ground to doing it right above and up from the skies. Frankly, it has always been more enjoyable and interesting for me to look at them from the ground. I don't know, maybe because it was far and inaccessible. And going through it now, it's beautiful again but not as mysterious as it can be from the ground.

As soon as we landed, we went to the hotel. I had to rest because the busy workday would start in the morning.

We were already at the local Business Center at 9am, where we were already waiting for the presentation. We were in negotiations for about two hours, and since the director had to go to another meeting for 2 hours, we had two hours break.

"As if it happened just for us, let's go for a walk," I began happily.

"I have no desire at all," was his reply.

"We have two hours, we are in the center of Rome, do you know how many beautiful things we can see?" I tried to persuade him.

"Well, I don't think I'll see something here that would surprise me, so it is better to go to the hotel and sleep."

"But I want to go, and I want you to be with me," I said sadly.

"Even if you try, you won't convince me; we will meet right here in two hours. And you go, let's see what you will see, what you will find."

"As you wish," I said to him sadly, and we left the business center in different directions.

Rome reminded me of Shakespeare's stories; every building seemed to tell its own story.

Of course, it would be nice if my walk was not alone, but maybe I needed that rest, which, however, did not last long. I felt that someone was always following me, but no matter how much I looked back, I didn't see anyone, so I began to ignore that feeling.

In the corner, I saw a beautiful shop selling interesting souvenirs. Since I saw a beautiful bracelet among them that I liked, I approached and began to look at it. It's a pity that I left my wallet at the hotel.

I was about to leave the store and lean into the corner of the building when I suddenly touched someone. My bag fell, and I apologized and went down to pick it up. And it was only while going back that I noticed how he handed me the bag and said:

"In fact, our meetings should always be with clashes."

I tried not to believe in my ears for a moment, but when I raised my head, I was frozen for a moment.

"Is silence a sign of agreement?" he continued smiling.

"I'm glad to see you here, too," I began, trying to keep the conversation going.

"I can judge by your surprised look that it is very unexpected," he continued.

"Well, I never predicted the frequency of our corner collisions," I said with a smile.

"And I knew it would be like this."

"You should have warned me during our last meeting."

"Well, I didn't know that before you left."

"Interesting; if I leave now, what other predictions will you have?"

"It is better not to try."

"Why?"

"Well, you said you were surprised and did not expect this. Do you want to experience such a surprise again?"

"Finally, there is something where I can agree with you," I replied with a smile.

"And I think you will agree if we have coffee in that small cafe and tell what has changed during this one year."

"Unfortunately, now my time is limited."

"More limited than last time?"

"More significantly."

"How many hours do you have?"

"My meeting will start in about an hour, and I have not seen anything here yet."

"So limited, huh?" he said, putting his hand on his snout as if thinking of something, and continued, "Well, I suggest a good solution so that we both will agree. I'll get some coffee from that cafe now, and we'll talk while walking. As a result, we will both have coffee with each other, you will see the city with a guide like me, and we will know what has changed in our lives. Do you agree?"

"You're excellent at arranging," I said with a smile.

"Then wait, I'll be right now," he said, running to the cafe across the street.

While waiting, I was still shocked by what just happened and went again into my thoughts. In a few minutes, he was back with two coffees in his hand.

"Well, let's move," he began, handing me the coffee.

"Sure," was my answer.

"Wait," he continued, "I have forgotten something."

"What?" I wondered.

"This is for you," he told me and gave the exact same bracelet I was looking at the store.

"But how?" I asked with a surprised face.

"I just thought you must have a souvenir from Italy".

I smiled. He really read my thoughts.

We started to walk. We were silent for a few seconds. Under the guise of drinking coffee, I preferred not to speak. But it did not last long.

"Well, then tell me, what are you doing here?" he began.

"Business meeting."

"Is it your business?"

"Yes!"

"Have you done it in a year?"

"Yes, as soon as I've returned from the journey."

"In fact, I made a good impression on you," he tried to ingeniously.

"I would say I had a good rest; that's why everything worked out," I said, trying to divert the topic.

But I realized that he was the main reason for my success because it all started with the desire to forget him and his motivating words. But he should never know that.

"In any case, I'm happy for you. I never doubted you would succeed," he said sadly.

"Thank you. I know you have always believed in my strength. Well, tell me, what have you achieved?"

"I am in the same business as last time, but the workload has increased, and I try to find interest in it and travel like this."

"Last time, you did not have the opportunity to say where you work."

"I also have my own company. We are more stable and have no such business trips, but we have a stable monthly income."

"Excellent, you are probably satisfied with the situation you are in."

"You can say that. Of course, there are always flaws, but I am optimistic," he said, smiling into my eyes.

"And I like that optimism in you the most," I said with a smile and looked into his eyes again.

We were talking like two close souls. I could see hidden and unspoken words in every word, but maybe it just seemed to me.

Here, we came to a beautiful monument, which was closed.

"It's closed, pity," I said in a sad voice.

"What would you do without me?" he said

with a smile and hurried to the other side of the building. All I had to do was to follow him.

It turned out that he knew the guard, so we managed to sneak in.

"So I see, all the doors are open to you," I joked.

"Unfortunately, not all of them," he said, looking at my face and running forward, reaching out to help me get down the stairs.

"Do you know what was here?" he asked.

"No."

"The greenhouse of the royal family, there were many trees and flowers, and in the center, there was a theater."

"And what is preserved now?" I asked

curiously.

"Only a corner is still in bloom, and I will take you there now."

We walked through a stone-built side and a glass-clad building from above, which smelled of antiquity. Being alone with him, it was as if I was starting to experience the same emotions again as a year ago. He was pulling me like before; the struggle with me was forcing me to come to that conclusion. One thing was clear. He was as close to me as ever, and it was a pleasure to be with him even in this antiquity.

"Here we are," he said, pointing to a part of the building covered with plants.

"It is interesting that it has remained like this

here," I continued.

"It is because of the place of the room, from the lighting, that antiquity has not yet finally ruled here."

"Is this also on the verge of extinction?" I asked curiously.

"Everything is on the verge of extinction; the question is when and what will last longer," he said sadly.

And there was silence again. We stood face to face in front of these plants and looked at each other as if we were longing. And when I felt that everything was getting deeper, I stopped and started by looking at my watch.

"My time is up."

"Yes, Cinderella, it's time to give you back," he joked in a sad voice and held out his hand to guide me to the exit.

We were already out in a few minutes, since I was late, all we had to do was run. It's good that he knew the way. Otherwise, we would have lost a lot of time before I got to GPS.

And here we were at the entrance of the Business Center.

"Did we make it?" he asked breathlessly as he reached the entrance.

"And we still have 5 minutes to breathe," I said breathlessly, too, and my boyfriend approached us at that moment.

After losing myself for a moment, I got myself together and started.

"Meet David, this is my boyfriend Felix."

I felt David's face taking a different tone when he heard what I said, but without losing himself, he reached out, gave his hand, and began.

"Nice to meet you, Felix."

"How do you know each other?," said my boyfriend Felix.

"From last year's trip," I began.

"It turns out we love to travel; what about you?" David continued asking Felix.

"Not so much; for me, it wastes time. I can

also relax at home."

"Clear. Well, it's a matter of preference," said David, looking at me.

"Well, we'll be late," I interrupted, wanting to end the conversation quickly and say goodbye.

"Indeed," said Felix; we were already saying goodbye when David intervened.

"What are your plans for tonight? You will want to try the most delicious real Italian food. I am sure you will starve until the evening."

"We will be so tired after this meeting that we will hardly leave the hotel," I said, trying to avoid the invitation and meet him again.

"And I do not mind, at least we will eat tastily; give me a phone, man, I will call, and you will tell me the address," said Felix, taking David's phone number.

I was surprised, but there was nothing I could do. Everything went against my plans.

I felt like I was in the air during the whole meeting. I had no idea what would happen in the evening. And why is David here? Is destiny left unfinished things again? And most importantly, why does he keep pulling me so hard?

When we got to the hotel, the first thing I did was go shopping and order a terribly strong coffee so I could get ready to face the evening meeting.

I was in line at the cafe when suddenly I saw a little friend sitting alone in the corner with his dog. I approached with a smile and started.

"Oh, I missed you so much."

"Good," was his short answer

'"Well, what are you doing here? Are you traveling again?" I asked.

"Yes!"

"That is interesting? You are the second person in my life with whom destiny constantly meets me. Well, not counting the dog."

"And who is the other one?" asked the boy.

"Do you remember the boy from the roof?"

"The one that you liked?"

"You can say so. Yes, he is also here. And I can say that I didn't see both of you at the same time, and here we are; I see you both in the same place. It is an interesting coincidence."

"I told you he is a good one," said the boy.

"You told me so, even though I do not understand why you are so sure if you do not know him."

"I know."

"How?"

"'From the roof."

"Well, yes, I know him from the rooftop, but you haven't communicated, have you?"

"There was no need for that," the boy said confidently.

"Well, I do not know how it is with you children, but we, adults, can't recognize someone until we communicate."

"And do you already know him?"

"It seems so to me. He is gentle, caring,

interesting, a little bit crazy, and witty, and, as I understand it, he loves to work and travel."

"And he is good," the boy intervened.

"Well, you can say he is," I said with a smile, following the boy's heart.

"Where is he now?" the boy asked curiously.

"He is getting ready for our meeting with me and my boyfriend in half an hour. Oh, I forgot about the meeting."

"Your boyfriend?" the boy asked with a surprised tone.

"Well, a lot has changed this year, and we have not seen each other, including that I already have a boyfriend."

"Is he good too?" the boy asked.

"Um, if you tell me how you measure that, I will tell you."

"Is he gentle, caring, interesting, a little crazy, funny?"

"You are a cheater, you repeat my words."

"Is he good?" the boy asked again.

"Well, he is different; he is interested mainly in work, sometimes gentle, funny, and far from being crazy."

"No, it doesn't matter, the guy from the roof is better," the boy said with a childish smile.

"It's pointless to argue with you, I know, that's why I'll ask you again at our next meeting, okay?" I said, summing up the conversation.

"Okay."

"Well, I have to go. It was nice to see you again. I hope to see you soon."

"We will meet," the boy said with confidence.

And now, the time has come for me to fight my inner fears and temptations again.

When we arrived, he was already there and greeted us. The food was really delicious.

The conversation was mostly between Felix and David. It seemed they had some things in common about work and plans. I just enjoyed being silent and following the conversation. I was afraid to say or do anything extra, so I chose a passive "position".

Time flew by, and I became more and more convinced that something was wrong and that something was pressing inside me.

Looking at the two of them talking warmly, I was smiling inside myself... what is life, when every time you are faced with a choice and doubt... when what you knew was right for you, the next moment at once may seem to be wrong, or you may not understand anything at all... and looking at the two of them,  the only thing I wanted to do was run away. And, yes, I realize that I've chosen to escape again, but at least I will prevent myself from further inner questions and thoughts.

Escape... the easiest way for everyone... from every question, from every situation... the easiest solution... when you do not start demanding more from yourself, but run away from yourself, from your desires, from your memories... and thus not understanding what you are looking for, you hurt yourself and break you down again, go self-contained, without demanding more...

We left the restaurant and moved to a pub where, according to David, one of his friends was going to play, which would be interesting for us.

The environment of the pub was active and full of people. We settled on the sofas in the corner of the room with David's friends and immediately ordered a drink. Electro-music makes the brain stop. One more glass of wine, and it seemed I would break away. And nothing was more oppressive than David being by my side every second. He was influencing me in some inexplicable way, and I was somehow hardly protecting myself from his energy to be able to stay there.

Sometimes, we desire to break the beauty in us, the one that happens automatically... after all, that beauty is uncontrollable... and we must be as strong as possible so that the beauty does not win...

I could not stand it anymore, and David was already feeling the fluctuations of my gaze; he was behaving so simply that if I hadn't recognized him, I would have thought he was just spending time. Still, something was telling me this was not the end.

He looked at me regularly while speaking, perhaps feeling my anxiety, unlike Felix, who was already accustomed to the environment and to David's friends, with whom he had already established business relations.

I couldn't stand it anymore, so I apologized and tried to find some fresh air. Of course, David didn't look indifferent and saw how I was going. And behold, I saw the stairs going up, and there was no sound. I got up and tried to take a deep breath. It was dark. Quiet. Empty. Ideal place. I closed my eyes and was enjoying the silence when I heard.

"Are you running away again?"

I opened my eyes, confused, and seeing David, I tried to divert the topic.

"I've drunk a lot of wine."

"Oh, that wine. It always makes us want to run away," he joked.

"So, who did you run away from?" I continued, not wanting him to come closer.

"I have come to find you," he said in a sad voice, looking into my eyes with that deep look.

My response to him was not long in coming.

"And what do you want from me?" I continued after the silence, and the effect of alcohol was the reason for my bold counterattack.

"Have you not guessed yet?" he continued.

"I want to hear that from you," I said,

smiling and joking.

He smiled. I felt that he was hesitant in his thoughts and needed time to formulate his thoughts.

"Imagine walking through the dark streets, necessarily with headphones and listening to your favorite songs, and people are like little figures, you can read a story on everyone's face, which is unique and so simple... and at that moment you look around, look for something that is unpredictable and makes you think endlessly... trees, wind, stars, the moon, which is slowly hiding in a veil, forcing your thoughts to go with it," he began after the silence.

"And what thoughts does it evoke?" I asked.

"I won't let you hide any more," he said, staring into my eyes.

"What?" I asked, wishing I did not understand what he meant.

"Yes, I have finally understood myself, and I am not searching anymore!"

After these last words, I had two things left to do. Either tell him what I feel whenever I see him or divert the topic again and run away.

We all want someone to fight for us, compete, capture, persuade, prove, show, and make us feel... There is a feeling inside all of us that pushes us to feel the need for someone, the one we will love, the one who will love us in return, the one who will hug and never let us go, with whom you can talk whenever you want and about whatever you want, who will understand you even when every word you say sounds like a delusion, whose touch sparks an energy strong enough to make every moment feel purposeful... we all want it. Still, few of us allow it to be...

"Have you ever felt that you didn't want to be what you are?" I began working out a tactic.

"Many times," he answered.

"What do you want to be?"

"Any animal."

"Why the animal?" I asked.

"They are more free, more sincere, and everything is easy for them. And what about you?" he continued.

"A Bird... I have always wanted to be a bird... to go wherever I want, whenever I want and every time, waving my wings, to take a deep breath and feel inner peace and harmony."

"And you are a bird to me now," he said, holding my hand.

"Why do you think so?" I asked, looking worriedly at his hand.

"You always run, fly away, when you feel something approaching you," he said, gently raising his hand to my face and continued, "forgive me".

"For what?" I asked, looking at his look coming closer to me.

"For what I have to do now."

After his last word, he quickly turned his head towards me and kissed me. It was like an explosion... inner... emotional... and I first tried to resist. Still, I gradually felt an inner calm and a strange attraction to him. I wanted to feel him endlessly. But not everything was so easy. And the effects of alcohol tripled my emotional freedom.

He slowly removed his lips from my lips, holding my face with his hand.

Coming out of shock, I only understood that nothing else would be as it was.

"Forgive me," he repeated again, leaning his head on mine.

"I don't want to understand what you have done now," I said in a sad voice.

"I already want you to understand; I feel and know you too. I do not understand why you are still playing," he said, continuing to caress my face.

"It's wrong," I continued.

"What?" he said.

"We," I said.

"We can finish it right," he continued.

"You do not understand, it is not right, I can't," I said, leaning my head on him.

"Why can't you? I don't understand you, honestly," he said, a little irritated, raising his head.

"You will think I am crazy. I can't say, I'm sorry, I can't," I said, running away from him and hurrying down. He ran away after me, and I heard him calling me several times.

As I approached our table, I told Felix that I didn't feel good because of drinking and wanted to go to a hotel. Saying goodbye, we left. Of course, all David had to do was watch how we were leaving.

Some people say what is not what they feel..., and some are silent about what they feel... It is difficult to say who I belonged to at that moment, but one thing was certain. Either way, neither you nor he will ever understand what you want...

Arriving at the hotel while watching TV on the sofa, I turned to Felix and started.

"Would you please give me your hand for a minute?"

"What do you need it for?" he said with a strange and surprised look.

"I just want to hold it," I continued.

"Take it, just don't stop me from watching the movie," he said, extending his hand to me.

I held it tight. My only wish was to try to feel one or more of what I felt when I touched David's hand. It seemed like a measure for me, a touch that would say everything. After all, so much can be understood from that touch.

And no matter how much I tried to concentrate and feel, I didn't feel anything. It was empty, with no spark. That was the difference. Why do I have to focus on feeling something?

Leaving his hand, I said I wanted to breathe fresh air and climbed to the hotel's roof.

It is interesting that whenever our thoughts are mixed and we need to think, we look for a higher place. It is as the higher you are, the louder your thoughts are, and we begin to understand everything. And of course they will be heard from the 13rd floor.

I was standing on the very edge of the roof, from where the light-covered city was opening down, and above, the golden stars and the moon, which were the same as every night and seemed to be the only thing left in this world that I was sure of... the most valuable... same as during the night in a tent, street walk, return…

There are moments when there is silence inside, even when there is unbearable noise outside... and if we go deeper, such moments have a peculiarity of being repeated. The only difference between today and tomorrow is what is in your head today to see tomorrow before your eyes. And most of all, I am afraid of my dreams - which come true…

Ah, if only I could tell him that the only reason I ran away from him was a dream I had on the day of our "first encounter"... which seemed to predict what would be, how it would be, where it would take…

Have you ever had your dream so clear and emotional that you confuse it with reality? It is as if you live every moment, feel, resist, and enjoy... but opening your eyes, you find yourself in a completely different reality, which, however, is still only a part of a dream, and, even after opening your eyes, appearing alone, feeling cold, you have to fight and only when you hear a loud noise, understand that the noise comes out of the dream, from "the real reality". And only by waking up a second time you wake up. Dream in a dream. This is the reality I lived every night after meeting you.

How could I tell him that I was afraid of him?! And that I was afraid that a dream would be right, that we would always become strangers... I could see our path and our separation and, unfortunately, my dreams were always right; they always became a reality... the only solution was to hide... to hide from desires, hide the feeling inside.

People like to hide... to hide from their feelings, their thoughts, their admiration... it makes them "to adapt" to the environment, "to adapt" the inner world to what is happening in the outer world, sometimes to be silent, sometimes to laugh even when what is happening does not seem worthy to laugh from the inside... sometimes to weaken, to be weak, even it is done only for not frightening the other person... sometimes to take the status of a victim, to understand who will be by your side when you are alone and to feel the need for someone, even if you are so strong inside that your strength never leaves you alone... sometimes to sing a completely different song, even inside it is a completely different melody... calmer, more peaceful, more fairytale... but sometimes hiding gets more. After all, no one can predict you like that... and when the time comes, the stage of self-analysis and understanding of the environment ends. You start to act and surprise, succeed, and achieve your goal... this way, you are small, vulnerable, and the weak "self" is always under protection... and only you protect it, hiding from everyone...

And if you were here now, you would mix all my selves, all my insides upside down, you would draw all my energy, giving yours, the positive, the strong, the inspiring one... and I would enjoy you again, but again letting you go because it was as if the loud bangs in my head were telling me to let you go.

And now, standing at this height, holding my head firmly, I only want to say, why does my inside dance only when I touch you?

And, if you were here now, I would apologize to you for all that I did or did not do, but it wasn't the real me. I would say that I am stupid, that I was running away from you, that I believed in my dream, that I did not believe in you, that I did not tell you all my fears and secrets. Ah, if only you knew all my fears... and you are the only one who would understand them. I have finally realized that the only thing that deprived me from you was the fear of getting attached to you and becoming weak.

At that moment, I had an insatiable desire to return to the pub. Since it was near our hotel, I quickly descended and started walking towards it. I went inside. The crowd was still there, but I could not find him, no matter how hard I tried to look for David's face in everyone. His friends were there, but he was not. Realizing he was no longer there, my stay was useless, so I sadly returned to the hotel.

It was pointless... one mistake, and I ended it all before even starting; I crushed him, broke him, and the courage he had in kissing me, even in the presence of Felix, has changed from my response.

And, behold, I'm already on the plane... What about him? I'll never know where he was at that moment.

After each of our journeys, something changes in us; in this case, the fear of putting me in the status of an endless victim has changed. I was not afraid of anything else... but the only thing I wanted and could do without fear, I could not do anymore.

Days passed. I was busy again, and it made no sense to continue my relationship with Felix. No reason to continue an emotion that is not blooming as the one you already felt once.

Again, David, not even in my life, motivated me to move forward and achieve new success in my business. I could feel his presence everywhere. Sometimes, it turned into schizophrenia when I looked around and felt like he was with me. Of course, that was not real, and it was just the result of my desire and imagination. But, oh yes, that was what made me not feel alone and to make the right decisions.

I wonder how a person can affect your whole being and life. When you change, and the reason for that change is a person who just did for you the things like the touch and the care, the one who just smiled with you, the things that you needed the most, the one who believed in you and gave you infinity. Simple things, and if we go deeper, they don't imply any complication, but they bring significant change.

Two months have passed since my trip. Things were going better than ever.

The motivation was surprisingly endless. I had a meeting with my friend An in the evening. An was the only one who knew about David and my actions.

"How do you feel?" she began.

"It's like starting all over again, on a clean page," I replied.

"Have you forgotten?" she continued.

"I think I will never forget. All I have to do is to do everything so that when one day we meet again, I can tell him that I am fine."

"And you do all this just to tell him one day

that you're okay?" my friend asked with surprise.

"Yes, because I know he wants it. I can't explain how I feel about him, even right now sitting here, his energy, his presence inside me, in my mind," I continued.

"I try to understand that, but by no means I can't understand that people have been searching for years to find what is right and when they find it all that remains is to dare and do something to keep it, and you do nothing."

"By doing nothing, I am already doing something. I do not run away from anything else. If our story is incomplete, it will continue somewhere, finding some reason."

"And until that …"

"Until then, I will work on myself, improve

myself, and be ready," I continued, interrupting her.

"You have chosen him as a "shield" that protects you from everything. You have the answer to every question, but which, I am afraid, will hurt you."

"I have already hurt myself, and no one can ever hurt me more than I did," I continued in a confident tone, "I feel something that still moves me even now."

"I just want you to move on and never look back," she said in a caring voice.

"I promised myself, and you will see it. Nothing will stop me," I said, taking her hand.

After our conversation, I decided to take a walk home. And since it was snowing outside, walking and thinking under the white was doubly fun. White, clean... At that moment, people looking up will assure you that such a feeling is soothing when you feel foreign bodies on your face falling from above, which at first give off coldness, disappear in the heat of your body, and then cause a feeling of freshness. And closing your eyes with your face raised, you feel inner peace. And that's one of those moments when you wonder why it doesn't happen so often in our lives. Maybe because we miss and always wait for it? This is how everything is in life: when something can't exist all the time, you start to miss it, especially when you get used to it and make it your own... you start waiting…

I was about to reach my apartment when I saw my friends playing near the same bench: the dog and the boy.

Approaching them, I started.

"Will you let me join your game?"

"Yes, with love," the boy said, throwing the snowball at me.

We started playing snowballs. With each blow of the snow, the dog jumped up and tried to catch them. I seemed to remember my childhood. After playing and freezing for a few minutes, we stopped, and the boy started.

"I want to play again."

"It's too late; it's time to go home," I said.

"We'll go, but let me ask you a new question," the boy continued.

"I listen," I answered.

"Did you see that good boy?" he said sincerely.

"Yes, and you were right as always," I said with a smile.

"I knew he was the good one."

"I found it out too," I said in a sad voice.

"Are you going to see him now?" the boy continued.

"No, I do not know where he is."

"I will help you find him," he said and got up.

"No, he will find me," I said, holding his hand so he would not go anywhere.

"Are you sure? I always find," said the boy stubbornly.

"I'm sure."

"Do you promise to be with him during our next meeting?" the boy asked.

"I will try," I replied, smiling, and heard someone calling my name.

I turned around, it was my friend.

"You forgot your phone inside the bar," she began, handing me the phone.

"Thank you very much. How good you are here. I'll finally introduce you to my friends, about whom I've told so much."

I said and turned to the boy and the dog. To my surprise, they were not there.

"They were just here," I said in surprise.

"They who?" asked my friend.

"The boy and the dog I was talking about. Haven't you seen them with me when you approached?"

"I only saw you standing here when I came."

"And no one was with me?"

"In any case, I did not see them. Is everything alright?" my friend asked anxiously.

"Yes," I replied surprisedly, and said goodbye and headed home.

They were there, but they were not there. Why did I always see them alone? Why did they show up whenever I was lost and in my thoughts? Am I crazy? Didn't they exist?

The questions were endless. The next morning, I started looking for the boy and the dog. Because every time I saw them in the same place, they were definitely from nearby, and someone other than me would have seen them and knew where they lived.

They were not seen in nearby cafes or street shops. None of the passers-by I know haven't seen them either.

I had no choice. The only thing I could think of was that they did not exist.

I was already reconciled to that thought when An, who saw my mental state, called me, and being a psychologist offered to meet in the cafe in the evening to talk.

And here we were in the cafe. She has started asking her psychological questions.

"How long did they appear to you?"

"More than one year. And the first time I saw them was when I was on tour with you. 2-3 days before that," I answered calmly.

"And what were you doing together? What were they telling you?" my friend asked.

"Every time we met, we just talked. The first time, he told me about his and his dog's friendship; the next time, he gave me a castle, and we talked about the person who was with me then and the third time I met him during the trip, we talked about you."

"About us?" my friend asked in surprise.

"He was saying how cute couple you are, and I... and... so...."

"And then?"

"Then I saw him twice, when I had already met David, and we mostly talked about him.

He assured me that he was good."

"And did it work?" my friend interrupted.

"Anyway, after our conversations, I started to

pay more attention to David, and in my mind, I was thinking about him endlessly."

"Did he, I mean, they, in any way, influenced the formation of the relationship between you and David?"

"I do not know. Wait, let me think," I said.

After thinking for a few seconds, I continued, "I think yes, because after seeing him I saw David. Then, on the roof, if it had not been that boy, I would have left and would not have been able to see David. The next time the boy said David was good, I started thinking about him and comparing him. Yes, they certainly did!"

"It's clear," my friend said after listening to me, taking a deep breath. "There's a term in psychology that, instead of explaining in terms, let me give you an example of your condition. There are memories, desires, and small images sitting in the deepest parts of every person's subconscious, which are always invisible in front of their eyes. Still, a person sees and feels them from the inside. And very often, that feeling takes one way or another. But before I continue, I have one more question."

"Of course," I said.

"How did you imagine your life, starting from an early age? Home, family, children... have you ever imagined such a boy in your life?"

My friend's question got me thinking. I began to delve into myself, remembering what I thought about my future life. And finally, a fact came to me. Yes, I always wanted to have a boy and, yes, a dog. And maybe my friend was right that they were just an expression of my desire. After telling my friend about this idea, I waited for her conclusion.

"Everything seems clear and understandable. People perceive and experience things differently—what they strongly believe or vividly imagine in their minds can sometimes manifest in the external world. This isn't necessarily a distraction, though it can occasionally be risky. In your case, the purpose was simply to reveal your inner desire. Your idea was so powerful that you engaged in internal dialogue about it, seeing it even when no one else could—because, at that moment, it existed solely as a conversation in your mind."

"And what was its purpose? And why do you not see them anymore?" I asked anxiously.

"The goal was to show you something. In this case, some possible turning points in the future also worked "the internal instincts" because, in any case, they were your ideas, mostly led by you. Now, you do not see them because you do not need them anymore, and something has already changed in you."

An's explanation of the situation seemed completely realistic and scientific. Of course, I was surprised, but I understood that it is true.

At that moment, all I wanted to do was go home. As I entered the house, I saw a long-forgotten piano in the corner of the room. I was seeing everything differently.

And, yes, very emotionally.

When I touched the piano keyboard with my fingers and started playing, it mixed in a thousand times what was happening inside me... every touch on the keyboard seemed to answer a question, every sound was like unspoken words that were hidden and became audible... and the melody, which was automatically played by my fingers running left and right on the keyboard, was reminiscent of a bird feather that was constantly swaying, and the wind in the air did not allow it to reach the ground... and so on and so forth it was climbing more and more, touching the branches of the tree, the noise of the city march and the sway of the wave... but always dancing upstairs... as if it's time was not over... as if it had not reached the place yet, not found the place where it wants to be endless... and the seconds become minutes, the minutes - hours and finally the moment came when there was silence... and in that silence, the melody inside was the highest thing that could be heard...

Several weeks passed. It was already spring.

I seemed to find solidarity with myself. Everything went as planned. The only thing was that I finally felt my heart after a long time, which always kept me moving, but inside, it was sadness. That day, I had a great desire to go somewhere, a sunny place; the only place that came to mind was the waves.

I got in the car and drove there. It was

about 2 hours, and I was already there - the place where I promised to return. And since it was still mid-spring, the air was cold, and a gentle breeze blew my hair with a smile on my face.

Away from everything, I started walking close to the lake, remembering the last time I was there and when I wanted you to be there, too. But I have already learned not to look back.

An hour passed. I was still standing and talking to the waves. Suddenly, the dancing wind made me look to the right. In the corner, a young man was building a castle with sand in the same place as my little friend. He was leaning towards me with his back, so I did not see his face. But my curiosity to remember the moment with my little friends made me walk to look at the sandcastle.

"Hello, I'm sorry to interrupt; if you don't mind, I'll just stand here and watch how you build the castle," I began, slightly lowering my head to the head of the young man inside the big castle.

No sound.

"I'm sorry," I said again, thinking he didn't hear first time.

Seeing that there was no response

again, I decided to leave. And I had already turned to go when I heard.

"Wait!"

I turned around and, not counting that he could be very close to me, I ran into him.

"You?" I said in a surprised voice.

"Me," he replied.

"How?" I continued.

"As always, with collision. I missed our clash meetings, and as always, the look on your face hasn't changed. I love it when I surprise you, and it looks like this time is more successful than the previous one," he said.

"This time is different," I said, still surprised and continued thinking loudly, "No, it is again just my imagination."

"Do you think I could do that then?" he said, taking my hand and twirling me.

"No, you are real, but how?" I said, convinced that he was not my next imagination."

"I was on a business trip and decided to see how you are. But when I approached your office and saw you getting in the car, I decided to come after you. Of course, after coming for half an hour, I already thought it was not very certain where you were going, but I did not stop; I decided to go where you were going. And, behold, I am here. You can't imagine how nice it is to watch how you talk to the waves from afar."

"And why didn't you come closer?" I asked in a low voice.

"I did not want to disturb, and then this way

turned out more beautiful."

"And now?"

"And now I dedicate this castle to you," he said, not allowing me to continue.

"Why?" I said remembering the moment of "deja-vu".

"Because you chose it," he said and came closer to me.

"Me?"

"And I hope you will let me say goodbye to you here because I just wanted to know how you are, and I have already done that," he said and left.

"Are you sure you know?" I shouted after him.

"Know what?" he said, stopping and turning to me.

"Do you know how I am?"

"Have you forgotten that we feel each other? You are as I am now," he said, standing motionless, waiting for my answer.

"I forgot to tell you something during our last meeting," I continued, stepping towards him.

"What?"

"What I want."

"During the previous meeting, you did not know what you wanted," he said accusingly.

"Maybe, or maybe I did not know how to perceive it," I said, trying to open to him my hidden feelings.

"And now what do you want?" he said, taking one step towards me.

"All my life, up to this day, I have been

telling myself that I wish he were here, the one who would understand my silence, the one who would not let me down, the one who would understand without asking questions, the one who would look at the stars with me every day and would not get tired of doing it every day, the one who would find me everywhere, the one next to whom I would not feel the need for anything else... And here, after two years, I finally feel what I need. And again, I imagine our future with that boy and the dog."

"What boy and dog?" he interrupted.

"It does not matter; the thing is that I feel it, and I feel it with you. Forgive me for not understanding me for so long; I was afraid... of you... of how I felt... and you... you allowed me to do what I wanted, not realizing that I would not dare to do what I wanted so easily. And now, this moment is the only thing I want to have endlessly... just like this…"

"I don't agree," he continued, stepping closer to me.

"For what?" I said in surprise.

"For an easy end and this one day, because we can still get lost, but already with each other... get changed, holding hands... and today it may seem to you that everything is

fine, but, believe me, every further day together will be better," he said, and came closer to me, holding my face with one hand, and continuing, "because we are just ordinary people, no peculiarities, who want the simplest thing that we can have only together. And any choice we make together will be right. And I choose this right now."

After his last word he kissed me. In those few seconds, the energy I felt from all our meetings passed through me, which I was trying to escape because of my fear. I felt every spark that I used to refuse every time I was seeing him, every breath, every unspoken word, every moment spent in silence...

And now, as I walk beside him, no other thought comes to me... I feel perfect...

no question... no doubt... and already I see the future very clearly for which I am ready... with him... how good it is that you are here now…

* * *

The only thing I learned from this story was that sometimes, no matter how hard our fears overwhelm us, we have to try to suffocate within ourselves what makes us do something we do not want to do and what we are afraid of. After all, that is why many stories remain unfinished…

MESSAGE TO MY READER

Dear Reader,

If you are reading this, there is a high probability that you have read the book and you are interested in it. Some moments reminded you of a part of your life, some of your character expressions, and maybe it taught you some things...

This book is more than just words on paper—it carries emotions, questions, and fragments of thoughts that many of us experience but often hesitate to express. It is my first self-published book and

as you turn the pages, stories have a way of making us feel seen, understood, and less alone, and if this book does that for you, then its purpose is fulfilled.

The idea to write this book came to me when everything around me was erratic, in a fast run, when many loved ones were so engrossed in their fears that they got lost in the choices and opportunities. All I had to do was fix the facts... And the thoughts just went...

And if, after reading, you have a question about whether there are episodes from my life in this story, I will answer YES, that they make up only 3%, mainly in the form of analysis of the situation.

Thank you for picking up this book. Whether you stumbled upon it by chance or sought it out with intention, I believe that stories find us when we need them the most. Your time, your thoughts, and your presence as a reader mean more than words can express.

I'd love to hear your thoughts! Share your review with me on Instagram and leave your opinion on Amazon—it will inspire me to create more stories for you.

Feel free to visit my website to explore more of my work and subscribe for updates on future books. I hope, in some way, I've connected with you. Until we meet again in another story…

www.lianaenli.com

With gratitude,

ENLI

www.ingramcontent.com/pod-product-compliance
Lightning Source LLC
Chambersburg PA
CBHW021149130626
46554CB00005B/1723